W9-COX-149

This book belongs to:

Disney's Out & About With Pooh
A Grow and Learn Library

Published by Advance Publishers

Written by Ann Braybrooks
Illustrated by Arkadia Illustration Ltd.
Designed by Vickey Bolling
Produced by Bumpy Slide Books

ISBN:1-885222-69-6
10 9 8 7 6

From the moment the sun came up, things had started to go wrong for Pooh's friend Eeyore.

First, a big gust of wind whooshed through his Gloomy Place in the forest and blew down his house.

“Why should I be surprised?” he said to no one in particular, staring at the pile of sticks on the ground. “These things always happen to me.”

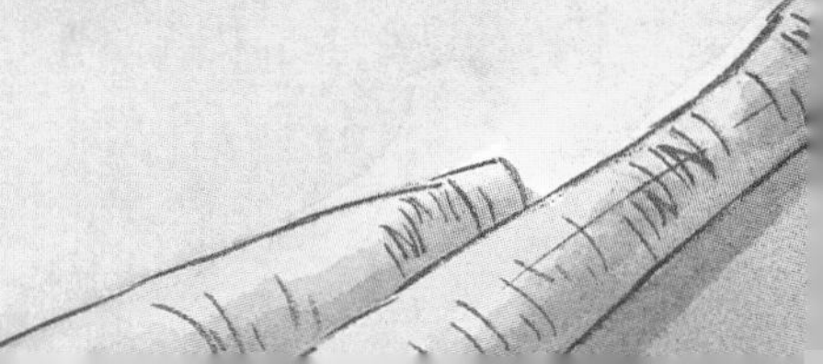

Then the poor donkey couldn't find a single thistle to eat. "No house," he muttered. "No breakfast. Oh, well. Maybe I'll find something by the stream."

But Eeyore did not find any thistles by the stream. Instead he found mud.

"Oh, dear," he said as he sank farther and farther into the muck. "This day is worse than I thought."

Fortunately, Pooh wandered by.

"Hello, Eeyore," said Pooh. "Are you stuck?"

"Yes, Pooh," said Eeyore. "If you're not too busy, would you mind helping me out?"

Pooh hurried to get a long stick. Then, huffing and puffing, he pulled Eeyore out of the mud.

“Are you all right?” Pooh asked his friend.

“Not really,” said Eeyore. “I’m having an awful lot of bad luck today.”

Pooh thought for a moment. “I know a way you can change your luck,” he said. “Come with me.”

Eeyore was not sure that anything could help make his day better, but he followed his friend anyway. Soon they reached a patch of clover.

"Most of these clovers have three leaves on each stem," Pooh explained, "but some have four. All you have to do is find one with four leaves. Then you'll have lots of good luck."

While Pooh watched, Eeyore began counting the leaves on each little clover stem. "One . . . two . . . three," Eeyore counted out loud. "One . . . two . . . three."

Again and again he counted, "One . . .two . . . three. One . . . two . . . three."

Finally, Eeyore looked up at Pooh. "I've finished," Eeyore said. "There aren't any four-leaf clovers here."

"Well . . . then . . . try another patch," Pooh suggested. "While you're looking, I'll go ask Christopher Robin how to look for four-leaf clovers. He knows all about these things."

After Pooh hurried off, Eeyore roamed the clearing, looking for more clover. “There’s some,” he said to himself. Then he began counting again: “One . . . two . . . three. One . . . two . . . three.”

After a while Pooh returned with Christopher Robin, as well as Piglet, Rabbit, and Tigger.

"Eeyore, did you find one yet?" Pooh asked.

"Nope," said Eeyore glumly. "I would have gone home by now, but my house blew over in the wind."

"Poor Eeyore," said Christopher Robin. "Don't give up. We'll help you find a four-leaf clover."

So the small group of friends spread out, making sure not to wander too far from one another.

In one spot, near a tree, Pooh was counting out loud. "One . . . two . . . three . . . one . . . two . . . three."

Near the path, Rabbit was counting quietly on his fingers. "One . . . two . . . three. One . . . two . . . three."

Tigger bounced off, shouting, "Counting is what tiggers like best!"

"Tigger!" Christopher Robin called out. "Are you sure you're not bouncing on the clover, instead of counting the leaves?"

"Oh," said Tigger, looking down at a flattened patch of clover. "I guess I am."

Meanwhile, Piglet was still searching for a patch of his own. When he finally did find one, he settled down in the soft green clover and began to count. "One . . . two . . . three. One . . . two . . . three. One . . . two . . . three . . . *four!*"

"Four!" he squeaked in excitement.
"I f-f-found a four-leaf clover!"

Everyone rushed to see. Tigger rushed so fast that he bumped into Eeyore, and the two went sprawling onto Piglet's lucky clover.

"Oh, no!" shouted Piglet.

"Look, it's a three-leaf clover now," said Pooh, when Tigger and Eeyore had gotten up again.

"Sorry," said Tigger.

"That's all right," Eeyore said. "It's just my bad luck again."

“There must be more four-leaf clovers around here,” said Christopher Robin. “Let’s keep looking.”

So they began again, with each of them searching for a fresh patch of clover to investigate. Soon everyone could be heard counting to three — even Tigger, who tried to do a little less bouncing this time.

Finally, Pooh cried, “Come quick! I’ve found one!”

"All right, Eeyore!" said Christopher Robin when they had gathered around the tiny plant. "You must be the first one to touch it!"

Eeyore felt certain nothing could help him, but he didn't want to disappoint his friends. "Here goes," he said. "I'll give it a try." He cautiously put one foot forward and lightly brushed the clover.

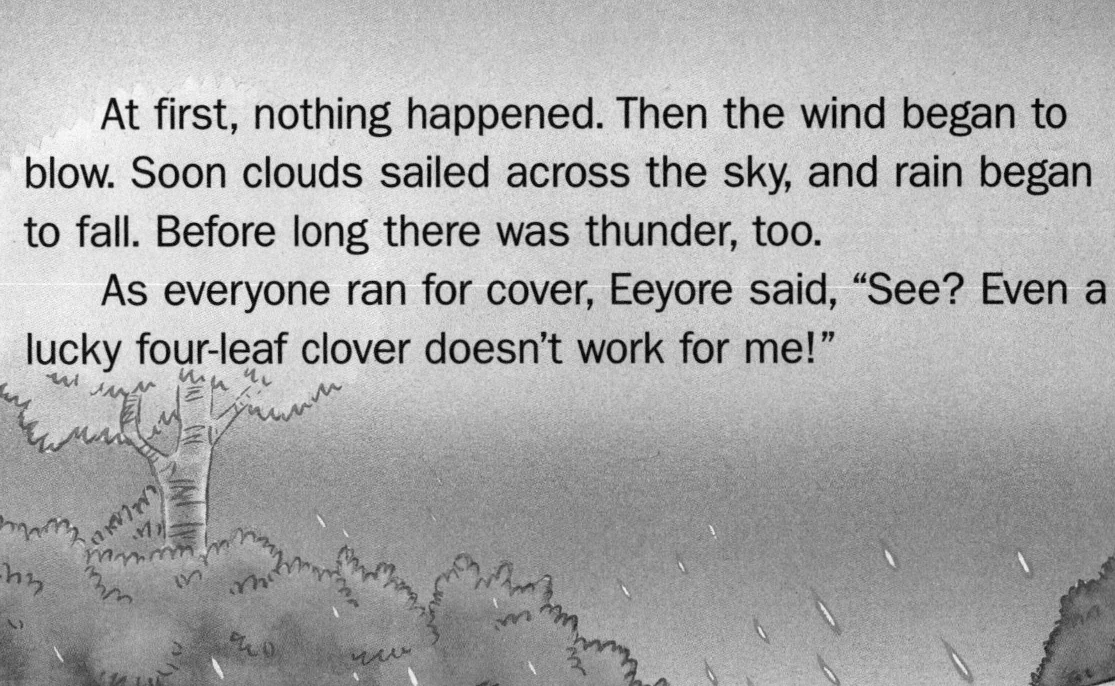

At first, nothing happened. Then the wind began to blow. Soon clouds sailed across the sky, and rain began to fall. Before long there was thunder, too.

As everyone ran for cover, Eeyore said, “See? Even a lucky four-leaf clover doesn’t work for me!”

The friends huddled together under a tall tree and waited for the storm to pass.

"Don't worry, Eeyore," said Christopher Robin. "We'll think of some way to turn your luck around."

The poor, sad donkey stared at the ground. Then he noticed there was something growing there. He bent down to take a better look. It wasn't clover, but it *was* thistle!

"Look," Eeyore said to the others. "Lunch."

"How wonderful, Eeyore!" Christopher Robin said happily. "Maybe your luck *is* changing."

"Do you think so?" Eeyore asked. And as he spoke, the sun peeked through the clouds.

“Look, the rain has stopped!” said Rabbit.
“And that’s not all!” said Tigger. “There’s a rainbow!”
For the first time that day, Eeyore smiled.

Christopher Robin whispered something to the others, then turned to Eeyore. "Why don't you stay here and enjoy your thistle?" he suggested. "We'll be right back."

Since he had missed breakfast, Eeyore was only too happy to remain behind. He politely waited until the others had left, then began eating. When he had gobbled up every last thistle, the others returned.

"Come on, Eeyore," said Christopher Robin. "We've got a surprise for you!"

Eeyore followed the group back to his Gloomy Place. But it didn't look as gloomy as it had when Eeyore left it that morning.

"A new house!" Eeyore said.

"Do you like it, Buddy Boy?" Tigger asked excitedly. "We made it ourselves!"

Eeyore was astounded. "No one's ever made me a house before," he said.

"Wait," said Pooh. "That's not all."

Eeyore followed Pooh and the others over to the stream.

Around the mud was a little fence, with a sign that said "CAREFUL. STICKY MUD."

"You'll never get stuck again," Pooh explained.

Eeyore looked at Christopher Robin, then Pooh, then Rabbit and Piglet and Tigger. He was not used to so many good things happening to him at once.

Finally he said, "I don't know if four-leaf clovers really work, but I know that I'm lucky to have you as friends."

"We're lucky to have each other," said Pooh.

"Yes, Pooh," said Christopher Robin as he patted Eeyore on the head. "We are."